Time for Bed, Sleepyhead

THE FALLING ASLEEP BOOK

DANIEL G. AMEN, M.D.

Illustrations by
GAIL YERRILL

ZONDERkidz

To Chloe, Eli, Emmy, Liam, and Louie and
all the little ones who need better sleep.
— DA

For my two wonderful children, Abigail and William, who
continue to inspire me, and my very understanding husband
Kevin who supports me through everything. Love you xx.
— GY

ZONDERKIDZ

Time for Bed, Sleepyhead

Copyright © 2016 by Dr. Daniel Amen
Illustration © 2016 by Gail Yerrill

Requests for information should be addressed to:

Zonderkidz, 3900 *Sparks Dr. SE, Grand Rapids, Michigan 49546*

ISBN 978-0-310-75822-8

Design: *Cindy Davis*

Printed in China

16 17 18 19 20 / DHC / 18 17 16 15 14 13 12 11 10 9 8 7 6 5 4 3 2 1

Time for Bed, Sleepyhead is a sophisticated psychological visualization game I played with my three-year-old daughter to help her get to sleep. It worked so well, we used it as our bedtime ritual for nearly five years, and I have shared it with the parents of many of my young patients.

Given the book's hypnotic nature, never read or listen to this book when driving, and never read it to a child to get them to sleep in a car. It may have unintended, negative effects on the driver.

The book contains powerful suggestions, having children stretch and even exhaust their imaginations to help tire them out. When reading the story, let it build to a crescendo of energy and enthusiasm, and then gently slow the pace to help quiet and slow the mind. If needed, you can customize the story to include animals, scenes, and people that fit your child's mind.

This book contains specific suggestions that help facilitate sleep. It is likely to cause some interesting conversations the next day. Be open. If you are a good listener, your child may begin to tell you more about their dreams and their internal life overall.

Daniel G. Amen, M.D.
Child Psychiatrist

"Time for bed, Sleepyhead!" said Momma Bear.

"Do I *have* to go to bed, Momma?" Little Bear asked.

"Oh, yes! Sleep is very important. In fact, it's one of the most important things you'll ever do! Did you know your brain actually cleans itself when you sleep? It's almost like your brain has a special cleaning crew that works all night long, getting rid of all the trash that builds up during the day."

"What happens if I don't sleep?"

"If you don't get enough sleep, your brain doesn't have enough time to clean up. Trash gets left behind. It can build up and get in the way, making it harder for you to learn—or even feel happy."

"I want a nice, clean brain, Momma!" shouted Little Bear.

"And that's what I want too! So, let's get you comfy-cozy, and I'll tell you a story that will help you fall asleep."

I want you to imagine yourself getting ready for a long, fun day at the beach.
Before we go, let's meet some of your friends who are going with us:

There is Eli, the young anteater.

Chloe, the soft, cuddly kitty.

Liam, the baby llama.

Louie, the lonely lion cub.

Aslan, the white German Shepherd puppy.

Emmy, the baby emu.

And, Shakespeare, the seal pup.

He is called Shakespeare because he likes to
talk so much and uses big words.

We load up our big van with lots of beach toys, towels, and treats. You climb in, along with Eli, Emmy, Liam, Louie, Chloe, Aslan, and Shakespeare, and off we go!

The ride is fun and playful, as everyone is trying to cheer up Louie. Chloe tries to sit on his head, and Emmy playfully nudges at his neck. Louie definitely is not feeling lonely today.

Everyone is so anxious to get there and have fun. The wheels of the
van go round and round and round. Will we ever arrive at the beach?

Aslan is the first to spot the beach. The sun is shining, and the water shimmers.
We park the van, and everyone climbs out and runs toward the water.

You jump in with Eli, Liam, Louie, Chloe, and the others right behind. You all splash and swim and play. Shakespeare barks out a funny song as he does tricks with the beach ball. The sun is hot; the water is warm. Everyone feels happy and safe.

Now, notice something really interesting—a minute for us here will seem like an hour on the beach, two minutes will seem like two hours, and pretty soon it will seem like you have been there all day long, playing and having a great time. Everyone feels safe, warm, and happy, even Louie.

Notice something else really interesting—any time you hear something besides the sound of my voice, you will hear it, but it will be a signal for you to become more relaxed, more comfy, and even a little sleepy.

After a while, you all get out of the water and head for the sandy shore. You and Eli, Emmy, Liam, Louie, Chloe, Aslan, and Shakespeare build a sandcastle together, making it bigger and bigger and even bigger. Next, you throw Frisbees. They sail through the air, flying farther and farther and … farther! Luckily, Emmy can run fast.

You and the whole gang play in the sun—running back and forth on the warm sand, racing each other until everyone plops down on their towels, too tuckered out to run anymore.

Now, after hours on the beach, everyone is very, very, VERY tired, and we all pile back into the van for the ride home. Everyone is feeling drowsy. Louie starts to fall asleep until Liam begins poking him. Liam loves to play and be silly.

Back at home, I fill up the huge bathtub with warm, bubbly water. You, Eli, Emmy, Liam, Louie, Chloe, Aslan, and Shakespeare all get into the tub for a soothing bubble bath together. It feels so good to clean the sand off. The water is so warm and relaxing. Shakespeare pretends he's not tired and splashes, but even he can't hide a great big yawn.

After the bath, everyone goes to the dinner table, but by now, everyone is so tired and sleepy, they are having a hard time keeping their heads up and their eyes open.

After eating, Aslan falls asleep next to the table. When Chloe is done, she cuddles up next to Emmy.

You are all so tired as you get ready for bed [*yawn here*], even your toothbrushes feel heavy. When you say your goodnight prayers, it is so easy for you to close your eyes. Everyone is so very sleepy. There are so many yawns [*yawn here*]—excuse me. I can't help but yawn too!

Your bedroom has a huge bed and the animals get under the covers with you. Emmy is nestled next to you on one side, Chloe is on the other. Aslan is at the foot of the bed, and Louie is not lonely next to Eli. Shakespeare is quiet now, sleeping next to Liam.

You feel so happy, but also very, very tired. Eli, Emmy, Liam, Chloe, Aslan, and Shakespeare are all drifting off to sleep. Louie is gently snoring. Even though you want to stay up, your eyes seem to close all by themselves. They won't open again until the morning, when your brain is clean and you are ready to have another amazing day.

Your animal friends, one by one,
begin to dream wonderful dreams:

Eli dreams of big, juicy ants, crawling on an anthill.

Emmy flies in her dream, soaring through the deep blue sky.

Liam dreams of basking in the sun in a big open field.

Chloe dreams of chasing a ribbon that you swirl for her in the air.

Louie dreams of playing hide-and-seek
in tall grass with his friends.

Aslan dreams about dog bones, lots and lots of dog bones.

In Shakespeare's dream, he happily floats,
balancing a ball on his nose.

And you, my love, dream of a very fun day
that you can have over and over again.

Good night, sleepyhead, good night.